Dear Parent:

Your child's love of reading starts here!

Every child learns to read in a different way and at his or her own speed. Some go back and forth between reading levels and read favorite books again and again. Others read through each level in order. You can help your young reader improve and become more confident by encouraging his or her own interests and abilities. From books your child reads with you to the first books he or she reads alone, there are I Can Read Books for every stage of reading:

SHARED READING
Basic language, word repetition, and whimsical illustrations, ideal for sharing with your emergent reader

BEGINNING READING
Short sentences, familiar words, and simple concepts for children eager to read on their own

READING WITH HELP
Engaging stories, longer sentences, and language play for developing readers

READING ALONE
Complex plots, challenging vocabulary, and high-interest topics for the independent reader

I Can Read Books have introduced children to the joy of reading since 1957. Featuring award-winning authors and illustrators and a fabulous cast of beloved characters, I Can Read Books set the standard for beginning readers.

A lifetime of discovery begins with the magical words **"I Can Read!"**

Visit www.icanread.com for information
on enriching your child's reading experience.

Library of Congress Control Number: 2022940752
ISBN 978-0-06-328331-2

22 23 24 25 26 LB 10 9 8 7 6 5 4 3 2 1 ❖ First Edition

Harold has a purple crayon.

But this is no ordinary crayon.

This crayon is made of magic!

Anything Harold draws
with his purple crayon
comes to life!

Look!

Harold draws a balloon.

It's a very large balloon.

Harold draws a string.

Harold grabs the string.

Hold on tight!

The balloon carries Harold

up, up, up into the sky.

Where is Harold going?

Harold is not worried.

He loves a great adventure!

Oh, no!

Harold is too high!

Pop goes the balloon!

Now Harold is falling!

Harold holds his purple crayon.

He starts to draw a soft cloud.

Hurry, Harold!

Poof!

Harold lands on a fluffy cloud.

The cloud sinks down.

Now Harold is stuck in a tree!

Harold draws a little ladder.

Harold climbs down the tree.

Harold steps onto the forest floor.

Harold looks around the forest.

It is beautiful!

Harold sees his friend Moose.

Hi, Moose!

Moose is silly and hungry.

Moose is looking for some sweet pies
to eat.

Harold wants to help Moose.

Harold always helps friends in need.

He uses his crayon to draw a pie.

Moose eats the pie.

Yummy!

Harold draws another pie,

then another, then another!

Moose eats all the pies!

Moose eats so many pies,

his belly grows big and wide.

Delicious!

Harold is tired of drawing pies.

He sits on a mossy rock.

Harold wants to relax.

Ouch!

Something sharp pokes Harold!

What did Harold sit on?

It's Harold's other friend, Porcupine!

Porcupine smelled the fresh pies.

She knew her friends were nearby!

Porcupine is very smart.

She uses her brain to help

friends in sticky situations.

Like right now!

The rock Harold is sitting

on is not a rock.

It's a big sleeping bear!

The sleepy bear doesn't see Harold!

But it does see Moose!

The bear walks toward him.

Porcupine trots in front of
the bear and shakes her body.
Sharp quills fall to the ground,
right in the bear's path!

Yee-ow!

The bear steps on the sharp quills.

It is time to escape!

Harold feels sad for the bear.

Harold pulls out the quill.

Then he draws a bandage

on the bear's paw.

The bear smiles at Harold.

It's time to go home!

Harold draws a door.

This will take them back home.

All three are safe!

They laugh and smile.

Harold loves adventures.

He loves his friends even more.

Harold and his friends

make a great team!

What adventure will they go on next?

This is Harold.

Harold is a curious boy.

He lives in a curious world.

If Harold can dream it,

Harold can create it.

HAROLD
and the
PURPLE
CRAYON

Meet Harold!

Adapted by Alexandra West

Illustrated by Walter Carzon

HARPER
An Imprint of HarperCollinsPublishers